SOME SORT
OF UGLY

NATHAN
GRAZIANO

MARGINALIA PUBLISHING
NORTH HOLLYWOOD, CALIFORNIA

Marginalia Publishing
North Hollywood, CA 91601
marginaliapublishing.com

A previous version of this work appeared on the
literary website Drunk Monkeys.

A portion of the proceeds from this book will be donated
to the following organizations:
    Children's Literacy Foundation
    International Labor Rights Forum
    PEN American Center

Cover photograph courtesy Kenny Lawrence
Book and cover design by Allan Ferguson
Author photo ©Liz Graziano

SECOND EDITION, FEBRUARY 2014

TO MY
FRIENDS
FROM
PLYMOUTH
STATE

CONTENTS

PRAISE FOR **AFTER THE HONEYMOON**

"*After the Honeymoon* is a clever, observant exploration of youth and its loss (Part I), alcoholism and addiction (Part II), marriage and its demise (Part III), and parenting (Part IV).... Graziano has a way of evincing distilled truth from every situation, and in language that feels just right for the moment.... The collection as a whole is resolute with strength and honesty."
—*Prick of the Spindle*

"Most of the poems are located within chaotic and troubled existences—lives of alienation, alcoholism and recovery, spousal violence, etc. I have a large amount of admiration for Graziano and his speakers who are determined to find meaning and beauty in the many faces of social dysfunction."
—*NewPages*

PRAISE FOR **TEACHING METAPHORS**

"Graziano effectively balances cool observation with dry humor, understated empathy and, yes, affection, for students and colleagues. Despite his self-deprecation, it's clear he works as hard at teaching as he does writing. He's serious about both. *Teaching Metaphors* takes a serious look at high school culture and teaches readers something about that world and, perhaps, themselves."
—*Concord Monitor*

"Sunnyoutside, a creative and prolific small press based in Somerville, Mass., has released a new book by poet Nate Graziano. Graziano is a mainstay of their list and for good reason. His work has the flashes of insight, irony, and humor as well as accessibility that makes for an engaging read.... Highly Recommended."
—*The Somerville News*

ALSO BY **NATHAN GRAZIANO**

FICTION
Frostbite (Green Bean Press, 2000)
*Chickenshits** (Green Bean Press, 2004)
Labor Day (Bottle of Smoke Press, 2005)
*Men of Letters** (Green Bean Press, 2006)
Hangover Breakfasts (Bottle of Smoke Press, 2012)

POETRY
A Night at the O'Aces (Phony Lid Publications, 1999)
No White Horses (Green Bean Press, 2000)
Seasons From the Second Floor (Green Bean Press, 2001)
Not So Profound (Green Bean Press, 2003)
*Idiot Warriors** (Green Bean Press, 2004)
Honey, I'm Home (sunnyoutside, 2005)
Teaching Metaphors (sunnyoutside, 2007)
After the Honeymoon (sunnyoutside, 2009)

* with Dan Crocker

PROLOGUE
WHAT'S IN A NAME?

I AM HAM. HAM, I AM. My full name is Hamlet Burns. My father, whose reading consisted solely of box scores and obituaries, was sold on the name Hamlet when he read about the death of a drama teacher who also acted in community theaters. I'm still unsure whether or not my father knows he named me after the anguished prince, or if he cares. My father is a small man, boisterous and stubborn, and my poor mother—who is one of the sweetest women to ever beg your pardon—conceded her first choice of name for her only child. My mother wanted to name me Mark, after the Apostle, but she didn't want to listen to my father bitch and went ahead with naming me Hamlet. My mom has always quietly enjoyed literature, which is where I inherited my own penchant for the written word. Nonetheless, by the time I left the maternity ward, I was named Hamlet, and the cards were already stacking against me.

Growing up outside of Providence with a name like Hamlet was an invitation for my classmates to tease me, calling me "Omelet" and beating the shit out of me. Some of the older kids in elementary school came up with the nickname "Fuck-let" but then got called to the principal's office for using it on the playground. In the fourth grade, my family moved to Warwick, and I wised up and started introducing myself as Ham, a small consolation.

But even Ham proved short-lived. In the eighth grade, I had an incident in gym class that christened me with yet another name that would follow me through high school.

I was crossing the monkey rings with my arms extended over my head when I spotted a group of girls stretching on the floor mats. I remember it clearly: I was wearing a pair of navy blue sweatpants and a black Def Leppard *Pyromania* t-shirt and felt my erection tent straight out against the cotton. The girls were the first to notice and started laughing and screaming and pointing at my sad boner. I closed my eyes and dropped like a sack of dead pigeons to the gym floor.

In a graduating class of 150 kids, only a handful used my real name. The rest referred to me by my nickname, the one that some of my old high school friends—to this day—still use. They call me Woodrow.

Although I'm not a bad-looking adult, I was a gawky and ugly teen; thinner than a bicycle spoke with patches of thick, purulent acne on my forehead and chin, and a shaggy brown mullet. Between my thinness, acne and the nickname, I would've gone my entire high school career with my virginity painfully preserved if it weren't for Carla Kay.

Carla Kay. What a wonderfully alliterative name for a girl who must have been, hands down, one of the easiest lays in Southern New England. During her freshman year of high school, her father, a town planner, ran off with a history teacher—a guy named Joe Cascione—and Carla subsequently went off the deep end with her daddy complex. At house parties, she would flash her tits for cash then invite guys to go with her into any available dark bedroom.

The girls at school were brutal to Carla, whispering and hissing and rolling their eyes whenever she walked through the hallways. It was mean-girl malicious and entirely undeserved. I sat next to Carla in geometry class, and she was always friendly to me. As a result, I developed a quiet crush on her.

Then one night after I drank a bottle of Boone's Farm at a party at Frank Menino's parents' house, I decided to approach Carla, who was drunk. After a half hour of babble and banter on the back porch, I went with Carla her into Frank's parents' bedroom. It took longer for me to figure out how to put on the condom than the actual act itself. Afterwards, she sat on the bed with her shoulder slumped and smoked a cigarette as I pulled up my pants, ashamed.

"That was amazing, Woodrow," Carla said, jabbing me in the ribs with her elbow. "The best minute of my life."

"I'm sorry, Carla," I said, looking at her reflection in the bedroom mirror, the moonlight streaming through the window outlining her thin, almost-boyish silhouette.

"Don't be," she said, exhaling a plume of smoke. "It's just sex."

"Don't you enjoy it?"

"Not really," she said. "Sometimes, I guess, when I'm by myself."

"Thank you for this, Carla. I'm sorry I sucked."

Carla laughed and patted me gently on the back. "You know, you're a decent guy, Woodrow."

"I like you, too," I said, completely misinterpreting her offhand compliment as a declaration of interest.

After I slept with Carla, my crush turned into obsessive love, and I tried wooing Carla with verse. When I think back, these poems were planting the seeds for my life as a writer. Late into the nights, I wrote pages and pages of painfully forced rhymes dedicated to Carla and then slipped them, unsigned, into her locker the next day. I'd go on and on about her lips being like candy apples, her eyes sparkling like a mountain stream on a clear day, and her ears were, of course, daffodils sprouting from the verdant grass that was her hair—Carla had a punk-edge and once dyed it green. While my poems were terrible and clichéd, it was something for me to do when I wasn't masturbating recalling my forty seconds of magic during our one night of love.

One day, Carla approached me in the hallway. "Are you the one writing those poems for me, Woodrow?" she asked.

I choked, blushed and vehemently denied it.

"It's too bad," she said. "They're pretty good."

I never came clean with Carla Kay about the poems, nor did I sleep with her again. Instead, I started focusing my attention on college. I had decided to attend a small liberal arts school in The White Mountains of New Hampshire. I envisioned a promised land of sex, the antithesis of the wasteland of spank magazines and Vaseline jars that composed my adolescent life in Rhode Island. I began to study *Animal House* with an academic interest. College had been advertised as an all-out orgy, a place where I'd learn to talk to girls and discover my swagger. As an eighteen-year-old singularly focused on my own crotch, sex—not an education—was as good an impetus as anything else to get out Rhode Island, call a mulligan, and start again.

That summer I took Acutane to clear up my skin and started lifting weights, putting on a little bulk. I was prepared to kill Woodrow and reinvent myself as Ham the Man.

And Ham the Man, I am.

1992
MEMORIES OF REDMAN

WHEN I ARRIVED AT COLLEGE in the fall of 1992 I was shocked to discover that the women in my dorm weren't running down the hallways in their bras and panties, pillow fighting and jamming their tongues down each other's throats. From the way college girls were depicted in the B-movies I watched on *USA Up All Night with Rhonda Shear*, I was under the impression that getting laid in college would only require a minimum effort, and for some of the guys, this was the case.

I, however, was failing miserably.

While I knew in reality that most women weren't the sex-crazed vixens from the B-movies, I was banking on a combination of newfound independence and copious alcohol to loosen the ladies and do the heavy lifting when it came to getting them in bed. After numerous nights awake and alone in my dorm room, trying to figure the reasons for my ineptitude, I came up with two principal problems.

The first was my hair. Throughout my life, my hair—or rather my ambivalence toward it—has resulted in a series of hot messes on my head. I've never had a hairstyle that fits me, and these days—as I'm pushing forty and balding—I've decided to clip it off. But in 1992, grunge music was the rage, and the campus looked like some eugenic tribe of Kurt Cobain clones. And it was these guys who were getting with the girls. I, on the other hand, still had my mullet from high school. While the mullet would have served me well in the some of rural areas surrounding campus, measured beside my peers, I looked like a throw back to MacGyver—only uglier.

The second cause for my ineptitude, I concluded, had to do with a drinking problem. You see, less than an hour after starting to drink, I would be completely shit-faced and leaning against the nearest wall to keep myself upright, swallowing spit and needing to puke. On top of this, I couldn't piss in front of other people, and at most of these keg parties, guys would piss in clusters in some designated area of a basement. My bladder would be near-bursting with beer, and I'd have to leave the party to take a leak. This was *the* problem: I took myself out of the game before it started. I realized that no woman in her right mind would look at some scrawny freshman with a mullet, hunched over a trash can and heaving mouthfuls of cafeteria pizza, or standing in a bush outside of a fraternity house trying to take a piss, and say to her friends, "There he is: the jackpot."

So I endured the tales of sexual conquests from the braggarts in my dorm who were astute enough to buy flannel shirts and wear them over Pearl Jam t-shirts. Meanwhile, I brooded in my room, running my hand through my mullet and trying to concoct a plan of action. Thanksgiving break would be coming in a few short months, and if I went home without any sexual conquests to share with my high school friends who had also left for college that fall, I'd be cast as the same old Woodrow.

In an attempt to get things moving, I visited a barber shop downtown and lopped off the mullet.

One cold night in October, I went a keg party with my friend Pete, who lived two doors down from me in the dorm. This was not an ordinary keg party, however; it was a "rush" for a fraternity, Alpha Delta Delta. The procedure for this rush was simple: the fraternity brothers introduced themselves, the president talked a little about the fraternity while spitting his tobacco into a plastic cup, and then they rolled out the kegs and tried to use alcohol to lure prospective freshmen into pledging.

It worked.

Once the official rush was over, they let in the girls. Early in the night, Pete and I noticed a round-faced stocky girl standing by the keg holding two plastic cups.

"That girl is double-fisting," I said to Pete, pointing at her. She wore glasses, and her hair was long and oily with uneven bangs. Her shoulders were hunched, which gave her the gait of a calcium-deprived old woman.

Pete shook his head slowly. "She's not double-fisting, Ham," he said. "That girl is dipping!"

"I didn't think girls used chewing tobacco," I said.

"You obviously didn't grow up in New Hampshire," said Pete, a native of the state. "I still wouldn't want to kiss her though."

Three hours later, Redman—a nickname Pete gave her, although her real name was Dawn—was beneath me in my bed, her small, flabby breasts falling towards her armpits. While having sex, she made these throaty, guttural noises that sounded like Chewbacca.

Due to the amount of alcohol I'd consumed, I was unable to orgasm—or piss—and after an hour, wanting only to sleep, I stopped and rolled off her. "I'm sorry," I said, taking off the condom and tossing it into the wastebasket beside my desk. "I'm too drunk."

"Do you want me to leave?" she asked, squinting to find her glasses on my desk.

"You can stay here. I have the room to myself," I said. Through the luck of the draw, I didn't have a roommate. The guy slated to live with me never showed up in September.

"Are you sure?" she asked, seeming shocked by my hospitality. "Most guys tell me to leave."

The one-night stand was new to me, and I was not versed in its tacit rules, but telling a girl to leave seemed bloodless and mean. "I'm sure. Stay here, Dawn," I said. "Just please don't dip in bed."

The next morning, after she left, I walked down the hall to Pete's room. He had done his reconnaissance work the previous night and found out that Redman had also made a reputation for herself on the third floor of our dorm where she had acquired the nickname "The War Pig"—I'm assuming after the Black Sabbath song. She had apparently slept with half a dozen of those guys and a few on my own floor. Between Redman and Carla Kay, I figured that I had indirectly slept with half of my age demographic in New England.

Still, the next night, when I was drunk again, I called Redman and went to her dorm room. Too dizzy to see or screw, I ended up falling off her bed, my head landing in a wastebasket by her desk. I began puking. Luckily, her roommate was gone for the weekend. While dry heaving, I let out a fart that must've woken up half the people in her dorm. Yet Redman ignored it and rubbed my back. Maybe

I had misjudged her. Who, other than her dentist, cares if she dips? She let me fart and puke in her room, and she was allowing me to have sex with her. A bond was forming between us.

I continued sleeping with her for the next two months. We were beginning to learn the concept of convenience and never discussed the idea of being monogamous or pursuing a relationship. It was understood that neither of us wanted that. However, brazen in the fact that I would be getting laid later in the night, I drank easier and started to build a slight tolerance, although peeing with an audience was still a problem. Eventually other women would start to pick up on this newfound confidence, and a few different, moderately attractive women started to notice me.

Eventually, as people often do, Redman faded from my life.

A couple of weeks before the end of our freshman year, Pete brought Redman home from a party, and she urinated in his bed after passing out.

"You know," Pete said as we brought his soiled linens to the laundry room, "Dawn is a nice person."

"I know," I said. "I like her." I thought about maybe writing a poem for her, but I was moving on to new women, hoping to find that certain someone who was still elusive—and would remain elusive through most of college.

But I noticed my hair was starting to grow.

1993
PETE AND MY PETER

TWO WEEKS INTO MY SOPHOMORE YEAR, I received a disastrous haircut from a guy on the third floor of the dorm who owned a set of clippers. He was referred to simply as Drain-O. Rumor had it that he drank a shot of the liquid plumber on a five-dollar bet and nearly killed himself. He had tattoos of flames on his forearms, a long goatee that dangled to his chest, and spikes impaled through his tongue and bottom lip. It was impossible to determine his age but most people estimated him to be somewhere between 20 and 65 years old. While Drain-O shaved his scalp to the skin, it didn't deter me from allowing him to cut my hair.

Humming along to a Pantera song, Drain-O shaved the sides and the back of my head with clippers, leaving a clump of hair on the top that hung down over the shaved portions like a spider plant. I looked like the inverse of a balding man painfully trying to maintain a ponytail.

"Looks cool," Drain-O said as he stood in front of me and checked my bangs to be sure they were even.

I walked to the mirror on his closet door. When I saw myself, I bit down on my bottom lip to keep from crying.

It looked as if the top of my head was spewing. I was half-tempted to ask Drain-O to shave the rest, but I didn't want to insult his work. More importantly, I didn't want him to pummel me into a thin pulp.

I wiped my eyes and turned around. "Looks great. Thanks, Drain-O."

"Not a problem," he said. "Spread the word. Tell anyone who wants a haircut to get in touch with me. I'll do it for a bowl pack."

"I think my buddy Pete is coming up later."

"Cool shit," said Drain-O. "I call this cut 'The Cobain.'" Other than a straight crew cut, it was the only one he knew.

"Oh," I said and left the room, leaving a bud I borrowed from Pete, who was dealing to our dorm, on Drain-O's desk for payment. But I didn't bother to warn Pete. I didn't want to suffer alone.

After the haircut—and largely due to a sexual drought that was a result of it—I began a strict regimen of masturbation. But I added a twist. In order to make the act feel more realistic, I started picking out imaginary girlfriends and trying to remain faithful to them. This involved thinking exclusively about one girl while flogging it. Sometimes when the thought of another woman would slip into my mind, a sense of guilt, dishonor and melancholy would follow my orgasm. I didn't want to be the type of guy with a terrible haircut who cheats on his imaginary girlfriends.

While I did find some solace in the fact that Pete had to suffer through the same haircut, the main difference between Pete and I was that Pete was still handsome enough to pick up women, even with a spider plant haircut. With his pot-dealing career taking off, Pete had also stopped attending most of his classes that semester so he had the time to groom his hair each morning and make it look presentable. I, on the other hand, optioned for the baseball hat.

The one class that Pete did attend was a biology lab that we had together. It wasn't, however, Pete's genuine desire to be around beakers and microscopes, glass slides and protective goggles motivating him to attend. Rather, it was my imaginary girlfriend.

I had never spoken to her and nothing short of the spider plant catching fire on a Bunsen burner would've made her look at me, so I never learned her real name. But I called her Bella, nonetheless. She was a small, slim girl with black hair as straight as a line, a bronzed complexion and a tiny bump on the bridge of her nose, a slight imperfection that juxtaposed beautifully with her natural double-D breasts.

Every Thursday morning Bella would proudly display her tits in an array of tight tops and blouses. I confided in Pete—who was equally enamored by Bella—that she had become my imaginary girlfriend, and each day after class, before I went to lunch, I would run back to my dorm room and pleasure myself thinking about Bella. I no longer had the privilege of a room to myself, but my roommate had a girlfriend across campus, so he was never there, leaving Bella and me free to make torrid and sweaty imaginary love in the privacy of my own mind.

Afterwards, I would walk with Pete to the dining hall, content with my imaginary love-making to my imaginary girlfriend.

It was a warm spring morning when Bella's red tank top erected my first classroom hard-on since The Monkey Ring Rod in junior high. Pete skipped class that day, sleeping off a hangover, and while I was supposed to be examining a cell scraped from the inside of my cheek, I kept casting furtive glances at Bella's breasts. For the next ninety minutes, I tried to keep my boner at bay with thoughts about geriatric lovemaking, rearranging the Red Sox batting order, and sharp objects being lodged into my eyeballs and testicles. Once class ended, I sprinted awkwardly back to my dorm room.

I had my pants around my knees and was mid-stroke by the time I hit the bed. I imagined Bella straddling my hips, wearing a short black skirt, sans the panties. With her thighs tensing, she pulled the red tank top over her head and buried my face in her massive mounds. I took a breast in each hand and massaged her nipples between my thumbs and index fingers, nibbling on them like a gerbil. She moaned sweetly as my cock pulsed inside of her.

"Yes, Ham, yes. Suck on my giant tits, tiger," Bella whispered as her pace quickened and she worked towards the type of life-altering, imaginary orgasm that only I could give her. "I'm going to come." She arched her back and started rubbing her clitoris. "Yes, yes, you hulk. Right there. I'm going to—"

"Lunch. Ham, are you coming?"

"Oh yeah, I'm—"

The door was swung open—I had forgotten to lock it!—and Pete stood in the doorway, his mouth open. My entire body convulsed. It was one of those moments when time slows down to a trickle as the mind tries to conceptualize the tragedy at hand.

Distraught, I tried tugging up my pants. "OH MY GOD! I'M BEATING OFF!" I screamed.

For some reason, I felt the need to state the obvious.

Pete chuckled and closed the door. I lay on my back, covering my eyes with my arm. At this point, I realized it would be nearly impossible to finish. There I was: nineteen years old with a bad haircut, no sex life, an imaginary girlfriend, and a case of self-inflicted blue balls. It seemed like a reasonable time to kill myself. Ham the Man, I am.

But I didn't kill myself. Instead, I zipped up my pants, grabbed my hat and walked down the hallway to Pete's room. He was lying on his bed, thumbing through a *Playboy*. I kept my head down. "It was Bella," I said. "She wore a red tank top. I forgot to lock the door."

Pete laughed. "Don't sweat it, Ham. It happens. My mother caught me waxing the bean once."

"Really? What happened?"

"It was a Saturday morning and I thought everyone was asleep. I thought it was safe."

"That's horrible, Pete."

"I had thrown off the covers and everything. I was butt naked, cranking on it when my mother walked in my room to get my laundry. I was just about to shoot. Man, it was a bad scene."

"Did you blow?" I needed to know.

Pete shook his head. "Not really. A little dribbled out the tip, but most of it stayed bottled up," he said. "I heard somewhere that you can get prostrate cancer that way."

"You really should get in the habit of finishing once you start," I said.

"Want to go get some food? It's the baked macaroni and cheese today at dining hall," Pete said, grabbing his coat off the back of his desk chair.

"Sounds good."

That day we saw Bella at the dining hall, and Pete witnessed the red tank top for himself. After lunch, we both went back to our respective rooms and locked the doors. We didn't want to get prostrate cancer.

1994
FIRE IN THE HOLE

THE SUMMER BEFORE MY JUNIOR YEAR, I got a job delivering food for Giovanni's Pizza in Cranston, Rhode Island. One Tuesday afternoon, I remember driving back to the restaurant after delivering four large cheese pizzas to a six-year-old boy's birthday party. This was the same day of the infamous O.J. Simpson car chase through Los Angeles in the white Ford Bronco after he had been accused of killing his wife Nicole and Ron Goldman. All around me there was a sense violence and unrest—a dark cloud covering the cosmos.

It was on this day—while stopped at red light—that my penis hole began to burn.

When I got back to the restaurant, I rushed to the employee bathroom. On the way through the kitchen, my boss Rich—a pear-shaped man with a thin mustache and a heavy lisp—stopped me. Rich was one of those guys who talked incessantly about his "girlfriend," but no one at work had actually seen said girlfriend. Rich was also a huge Michael Bolton fan—he owned Michael Bolton t-shirts and once flirted with the idea of getting the letters *M.B.* tattooed on his shoulder. "You have another delivery, Ham," Rich said, kneading dough like it was Michael Bolton's strong buttocks.

"I need to use the bathroom." I hurried past him.

"Make it snappy," Rich lisped as "When Man Loves a Woman" played from a tape deck above the stainless steel table where they rolled out the pizzas.

I got into bathroom, locked the door and unzipped my pants. The tip of my penis was stuck to my boxer shorts by a clear sticky fluid, and there was some bluish-lint around the hole. After a few minutes of poking and scratching and prodding, I attempted to urinate.

A co-worker later told me that the entire kitchen heard me scream. It felt as if I were passing battery acid through my urethra. I clutched the toilet seat, my knuckles white, grinding my teeth. After a couple of small dribbles, I stopped.

There was a knock at the door. "Ham, are you all right?" Rich asked.

"I saw a spider. I hate spiders." I was buckled in agony, and, worst of all, I still had to piss.

"Well, hurry up. These people need their pizzas."

At the time, I wasn't familiar with the symptoms of an STD. I slept through health class in high school because I never imagined I'd be having sex, much less contracting a sexually-transmitted disease. But it doesn't take a medical expert to figure out that something is horribly wrong when your penis is dripping a goopy discharge and your urine feels like it is being passed from a flamethrower.

I delivered the pizzas, biting down on my bottom lip as tears streamed down my cheeks. When I returned to the restaurant, I told Rich there was an *emergency* and I had to leave.

"Why are you crying?" Rich asked.

"A bad break-up," I said. "Michael Bolton is really getting to me."

"I know what you mean," Rich nodded. "Michael understands what it's like to have loved and lost. Michael understands the pain you're feeling, Ham."

"I'm feeling real pain," I said. "It burns like hell."

I was living with my parents that summer. When I finished my sophomore year of college in May, I had transformed, socially speaking, from an amorphous lump of loser to something in the vague shape of a social human being. First of all, I declared myself an English major—very practical—and joined Alpha Delta Delta, which got me into the keg parties and into the game. But more impressively, I had my first real girlfriend—an Irish girl from South Boston with long red hair, a sprinkling of freckles on her nose and cheeks, and a loud, infectious laugh that never seemed forced. Granted, Patty wasn't exactly discriminate when it came to choosing sexual partners and had a reputation within the fraternity for sleeping with the brothers, but that was immaterial. She was of the female persuasion and had agreed—on her own volition—to become the first to don the title "Ham the Man's girl."

And, of course, the driving force behind my social strides was, again, my hair.

After enduring the spider plant until it started to grow long, by the summer, I could almost pull my hair back into a ponytail. In fact, sometimes I'd stand in front of my bedroom mirror, pull my hair back with my hands, and pretend I was a Latin sex god—gyrating my bony hips and licking my top lip, saying "*Bueno*" to my own reflection.

However, there was nothing sexy about my current situation. On the way to the emergency room, I made the mistake of stopping home and telling my parents. I was still on their insurance plan and needed the information. They were sitting in the living room watching The Home Shopping Network when I came in.

"I need to go to the emergency room," I said standing between them and the television.

My mother gasped and clutched her chest. "Dear God. What's wrong, honey? Are you all right? You didn't hurt yourself, did you?" She stood up and pressed the back of her hand against my forehead. "Oh, Mother Mary, you feel like you have a fever."

"Mom, I'm fine."

My father rolled his eyes. My old man—a lifelong Republican who worked for the phone company for forty years—had worn a crew cut since birth, and my long hair had become a bone of contention in the household. He was one of those loud guys that never modulated the volume of his voice. It didn't matter if he was in a church or yelling across a crowded store, he was vociferous in both his volume and his opinions. He looked at my hair, not my face. **"THAT FRIGGIN' GIRL HAIR IS PROBABLY GROWING INTO HIS BRAIN. THAT'S WHAT'S WRONG WITH HIM,"** he said to my mother.

My mother ignored him. "Why do you need to go to the emergency room, Ham-honey? Have you tried praying?" My mother held my wrist. "I can get my rosary."

"It's something else," I said, lowering my voice to a whisper. "It burns when I pee."

"IT'S PROBABLY FROM SMOKING GRASS," my dad said. I had also admitted, during a family get-together, that

I tried pot. Although I had become a habitual pot-smoker by that point, the idea that I'd "tried" it one time was enough for my dad to consider me both a drug addict and pawn in the liberalization of America. You see, the Hippie Movement had completely passed over my father, and he blamed every social, political or medical problem, worldwide, on marijuana.

"It's probably nothing," I said. "I'll be back in a couple of hours."

"We're coming with you," my mother said. "Just give me a minute to get my purse." My mother left the room before I could stop her.

Then I was standing in the living room with my father, who was eying my hair and shaking his head. "Dad, you don't really have to come."

"I BET THEY HAVE CLIPPERS AT THE HOSPITAL. ONE TIME I HAD A HERNIA, THEY HAD TO SHAVE MY NUTS BEFORE THEY OPERATED. MAYBE THEY CAN CUT OFF THAT GIRL HAIR WHILE YOU'RE THERE, YOU FUCKING HIPPIE."

"Dad, seriously…"

"MAYBE IF YOU GOT RID OF THAT DAMN GIRL HAIR AND STOPPED WRITING THOSE SISSY POEMS, YOU WOULDN'T HAVE THESE PROBLEMS. BURNING PISS. CHRIST, SON, SUCK IT UP. BE A MAN FOR ONCE IN YOUR LIFE."

Pointless.

I sat in the waiting room for two hours, getting up once to use the bathroom and screaming as the lava-like urine shot from my penis hole. When my name was called, my father stood up and slapped me on the back **"SEE IF THE DOCTOR CAN DO ANYTHING ABOUT THE GIRL HAIR, DOROTHY."**

I was cordoned off from my fellow ER sufferers by a thin beige curtain while I waited another forty-five minutes before the doctor saw me. He was a tall, lanky man without an upper lip or much of a personality. As I described my symptoms, he nodded his head and looked bored.

"Have you had unprotected sex recently?" He asked the question without inflection, as if he were reading it from a script.

"Just with my girlfriend," I said, neglecting to tell him that my girlfriend had slept with an entire Soundgarden cover-band who called themselves The Black Hole Suns and played frequently at The Rusty Hammer, an off-campus bar.

"Take down your shorts and let me have a look," the doctor said.

I slipped off my boxers and lay back on the gurney. The doctor put on a rubber glove and examined my prick, which had shrunken to the size of an elbow noodle. "It looks like you have some discharge. I'm going to run a few tests."

"What about the burning pee?"

"I'm going to run some tests," he said sharply. I'm sure I was not the first frat boy with a dripping dick he'd seen.

He opened the curtain and left. Meanwhile, I sat there cursing my crappy luck. Patty was only the fourth girl I'd actually slept with—who wasn't imaginary—and my first steady girlfriend. Some men go their entire lives, sleeping with hundreds of women, and never contracting anything. It started to occur to me that there was such a thing as fate, some cosmic card game being played in the backrooms of our shared human experience. Some men were always dealt aces, and others, like me, had to rely on bluffing, holding out for one card which may or may not ever land in front of you. Sometimes, as was my case, you get dealt a shit hand and have to face the facts and fold.

The doctor returned carrying a couple of small glass tubes and a six-inch Q-tip. He asked me to lay back.

"This may sting a bit," he said.

He proceeded to swab my penis hole with the gigantic Q-tip as I writhed on the gurney and screamed and nearly bit off a piece of my tongue. Afterwards, the doctor drew some blood, gave my balls a quick jiggle then disappeared again.

After the doctor left, I sat on a plastic chair beside the gurney, wondering what the hell I had. At best, the doctor would come back and tell me it was some strange fungus that a topical cream would clear up. At worst, my dick was going fall off, and I'd spend the rest of my life with catheter bag strapped to my hip, sexless and depressed.

He came back a half an hour later, looking down at a clipboard. "You have Chlamydia."

"I have *what*?" I asked.

"Chlamydia. You need to take penicillin for a week, contact all your recent sexual partners, and tell them to get tested. Any questions?"

"That's an STD, right?" It was my first. It was as if I had been initiated against my will into some sordid and filthy subset of society. Only dirty people got STD's. I wanted to weep, but I held back and tugged at my near-ponytail. There would be plenty of time for weeping later, I told myself.

"It's a common STD," the doctor said. "Aside from HPV, or genital warts, it's one of the most common among kids your age. Be sure to finish the antibiotics and use a condom next time. Most STD's can be prevented by good judgment and common sense." He then shoved the prescription at me and moved to the next patient.

I slowly put on my shorts, plaintively glancing one last time at my poor, infected penis. Aside from becoming a new initiate of the Society of the Sexually Transmitted Diseased, I now had the unenviable task of telling my parents the results.

My mother and father were watching the television mounted in the corner of the waiting room. They both looked at me as I entered. I stared down at my feet.

"Is everything all right?" my mother asked and braced herself like she was about to be slapped.

At that moment, I couldn't think of a lie. "I have Chlamydia," I whispered.

"WHAT DID YOU SAY? CLAMS? YOU HAVE CLAMS? WHAT THE HELL ARE THE CLAMS?" My father stood up from his seat, his hands on his hips.

I put my finger to my lips—my face was pale. The ten other people in the waiting room were now looking at us. "No, Dad," I whispered again. "I have Chlamydia. It's a sexually transmitted disease."

"Oh, dear God," my mother said with her rosary wrapped around her hand. She clutched her chest and began what would end up being fifty consecutive "Hail Mary's".

"YOU MORON! ARE YOU SEEING HOOKERS? SEE, ELLEN, I TOLD YOU HE WAS SEEING HOOKERS. ALL THOSE LONGHAIRS ARE SEEING HOOK- ERS AND HAVING FREELOVE AND SMOKING GRASS. NOW YOU HAVE THE CLAMS! WAY TO GO, DIPSHIT!"

I was experiencing a shrinking sensation. My father smacked me in the back of the head. **"THE FUCKING**

CLAMS," he said and shook his head with disgust.

After I came home from the emergency room and my father had exhausted himself screaming at me, I called Patty with the bad news. She was living in upstate New York with her parents for the summer, working as a waitress at a resort on Lake Placid. Her father answered the phone.

"Hello, sir. Is Patty there, please?"

"Who wants to know?"

"This is Ham, sir."

"Are you on drugs, son?" For some reason, everyone seemed to think I was doing drugs. Luckily, I was.

"No, sir. Drugs are for thugs. Right?"

"Shut up."

"Yes, sir. May I speak to Patty, please?"

Her father slammed the receiver against a solid object—a kitchen counter or his head. I heard him calling her in the background. "Patty, some loser who says he's your boyfriend is on the phone!"

Patty picked up. "Hello?" Her voice seemed to beg the question: *Which boyfriend?*

"Patty, it's me, Ham." Ham the Man with the Diseased Penis.

"Hi, sweetie. What's going on?"

"Is your father still on the phone? I never heard him hang up."

"Dad, hang up the phone!" There was a growl and a click. "What's wrong?"

"It burns when I pee," I said. Instinctively, I grabbed my penis. It comforted me to hold it.

"What!"

"I have Chlamydia, and the doctor told to me to tell everyone I've slept with lately, so I'm telling you."

Patty was silent then she sighed. "That's not good. Who do you think gave it to you?"

I cleared my throat and took a deep breath. Then I began speaking in a slow, clinical tone, dodging the question and explaining what I learned of the disease by looking it up in the encyclopedia.

"You see, Patty, men typically know they have Chlamydia within a couple of weeks of contracting it," I said. "They have symptoms like burning piss and clear, sticky goop dripping from the tip their dick. Females, however, often don't experience any symptoms. But it's far more dangerous for them. It can attack their reproductive organs, like a bacterial pit bull."

"Is that what happened to you?" Patty's voice cracked. She knew. I knew. We both knew she was responsible for the fire in my hole.

"Yes," I said. "You need to get yourself checked. Or the pit bull." I took a deep breath. "Jesus, Patty, I'm sorry to have to tell you this."

"I can't believe it. How did this happen?"

"We got dealt a shit hand, Patty. Bad cards."

"Are you sure it was me?"

"Listen, Patty, I have to go and try to pee even though it hurts."

"I'll talk to you later, Ham," she said.

"Give your father my love."

"I will."

We hung up, and I went upstairs to take my first dose of penicillin. I swallowed the pill with a large glass of water and waited for the fire to subside. Wounded and defeated, I marched toward the bathroom.

⊕

There was never a formal breakup between Patty and me. We simply didn't speak for the rest of summer, so it was mutually assumed that **THE CLAMS** had torpedoed our relationship. However, within days of being on penicillin, the fire was extinguished; the faucets were turned off and the dripping stopped. I was no longer getting laid, but the filth had cleared. I called it a push.

When I returned to college in the fall and moved into my fraternity house, I avoided Patty, and she avoided me, each of us harboring our horrible secret and private shame. Other than my parents and the doctor, Patty was the only person who knew about the fire in the hole.

But I wasn't alone. There was a guy living in the frat house that had contracted every nonfatal STD in the book, and I quietly considered him my confidant. People called him Trench Mouth, a nickname he acquired after contracting the disease by going down on a Jersey girl visiting friends for a weekend. It was highly unusual, seeing there had been relatively few outbreaks of the disease since World War I.

Trench Mouth's real name was Mike, and he was a slender handsome guy with dark hair and prominent features—bright blue eyes and a chiseled chin. Charming with a gift for banter, picking up women was about as challenging to him as washing his hands. However, he also got dealt a shit hands when it came to STD's. I knew, unless I wanted to end up like Trench Mouth—the object of daily ridicule—I had to keep quiet about Patty and **THE CLAMS.**

Patty and I were successful in avoiding each other until the night of my fraternity's annual toga party when she showed up wearing in a beige bed sheet and nothing else. At first, we did the adult thing and pretended like we didn't know each other, but as the night wore on and we continued drinking, it quickly changed.

The next thing I knew, Patty was in my bed with her legs spread and her hot breath on my neck.

"Do you have a condom?" She panted, grabbing my cock.

My erection bobbed as I leapt up from the bed and ransacked my bedroom for a condom. The underwear drawer where I usually kept one—just in case—was empty, likely thieved by one of my frat brothers. "I don't have one," I said, exasperated.

"Shit," Patty said, pulling me on top of her.

"You got that thing taken care of last summer, right?" I asked and was inside her before she could respond.

"Of course."

A week later, I woke up and walked groggily to the bathroom to take a morning leak. I stood in front of the toilet, rubbing my eyes. At first I couldn't get a steady stream. Then the firewater started making its familiar path through my urethra. I seized, squeezing my eyes shut. No. Not again. I screamed, clutching the toilet seat. When I got out of the bathroom, Trench Mouth was standing outside the door with a cigarette dangling from his lips.

"What's wrong?" Trench Mouth asked, grinning. "I heard you scream."

"Nothing," I said. "I saw a spider."

He lit the cigarette. "I know that scream. You got a case of The Nasties, Ham-bone."

I mumbled something under my breath.

"Get dressed," he said, patting me on the back. "I'll drive you to the infirmary."

I kicked the floor. "All right," I said and went to my bedroom to put on jeans.

Trench Mouth drove a rusted out blue 1978 Pinto, one of the last still on the road. The radio was broken, so the only sound as we drove was the clinking and chugging of four enervated cylinders. He had the window half-open, smoking a cigarette. "Your first time?" he asked.

"What do you mean?"

"With The Nasties," he said and shifted his eyes to look at me. "I remember the first time I woke up with the fire water. I had no idea what it was." He smiled—as if the memory was nostalgic, bringing him back to a time that wasn't entirely unpleasant.

"I got it this summer," I said. "The Nasties," I added. Admitting it to someone else felt liberating, like freeing a diseased ghost. "I got it from the girl I was dating and I ended up hooking up with her again at the toga party."

"And you didn't wrap it?"

"No."

"Man, I remember one time I got The Clap and the crabs from the same chick. Can you imagine what it's like to go to the doctor with both? He barely said anything to me. He wrote the script and gave me some lice shampoo and the little comb. There wasn't much to say."

"How many STD's have you gotten?"

Trench Mouth paused and seemed to be counting in his head. "Let's see. I've gotten The Clap three times, the crabs twice, Chlamydia once, and, well, you only get warts once. But I've never gotten herpes, thank God … what is that? Seven?"

I nodded and stared out the window at The White Mountains, quiet on the horizon. Trench Mouth offered me a cigarette, and even though I didn't smoke, I took it. I lit the end, coughed, then inhaled again and coughed some more. Halfway through the cigarette, I got light-headed. "If you don't mind me asking, how many girls have you slept with?"

"Fifty or so. Give or take."

I did some quick math. Trench Mouth had been with fifty girls and contracted seven STD's. I'd been with four and was already on my second run with Chlamydia. I shook my head at my shit hand. "I've only been with four," I said. "There's Patty and this girl in high school. Then there's another girl who claimed we did it, but I don't remember, and Redman."

"Is that the girl who dips?"

"Do you know her?"

Trench Mouth nodded and dragged on his cigarette. "That sucks, Ham. Some guys sleep with hundreds of women and never even get chaffed. Some guys sleep with one and get The Nasties. At least you can be cured with penicillin."

I thought about it, and he was right. My shit hand could be worse. "Thanks, Mike," I said.

"No problem," he said, putting on his blinker and turning into Dunkin Donuts.

"Let me buy the coffee," I said.

"You might want to try some cranberry juice."

"I'll stick to coffee," I said. "What's done is done."

"You're all right, Ham-bone. This is no great tragedy," Trench Mouth said and offered me a second smoke.

1995
PISSING ON MY OWN LEG
OR HOW I FOUND FICTION

I WAS MINDING MY OWN, making out with a beer mug at The Rusty Hammer when this girl—no bullshit—tapped me on the shoulder and asked, "Are you going to take me home tonight?"

I'd seen her at the Thursday night poetry readings at the Poor Man's Cup, a café where all the *artistes* on campus gathered. After I moved out of the fraternity house midway through my junior year and into a dingy room in a communal housing building, I decided to reinvent myself in the image of the drunken and tortured American poet. I had stopped hanging out at the keg parties waiting for some girl—any girl, really—to go to bed with me. Instead, I started posturing around campus with like-minded poseurs, each of us with a carefully cultivated image. For example, I was honing the Jack Kerouac meets Richard Brautigan image, a hippie meets road-grunge motif, rarely shaving or combing my long hair.

My lack of hygiene, however, didn't seem to matter to this girl, whose own hair was bobbed at the ears, shorter than mine. Tall and thin, she had a pale, bloodless complexion with a pronounced overbite. Still, there was something friendly and unassuming in the way she asked me the question.

As she stood beside me, waiting for me to answer, I looked around the bar, expecting to see a group of my frat brothers at the pool table snickering, or Pete sipping Guinness, pointing a finger gun at me—"Gotcha."

"You want to go home with me?" I asked, pointing at my chest. "Are you sure you have the right person?"

When she smiled, her bucked-teeth shone like torches through the bar smoke and her cheek bones rose, her eyes pinching at the corners. "Yes, silly," she said. "I've been working up the courage to talk to you for weeks."

"You're fucking with me, right? Who put you up to this? Was it Pete? Big Ray and Wiggy? Trench Mouth? Come on, what gives?"

"What are you talking about? I know who you are. You're Ham, and you're *a poet*."

I ran my hand over my hair which was pulled back in a ponytail, a pose I had practiced extensively in the mirror. I didn't want her to know that I was secretly thrilled to be addressed as *a poet*. Ham the Man, I am. I lit a cigarette—a habit I picked up bumming butts from Trench Mouth and had acquired as part of my image. "No bullshit?"

"I'm serious." She leaned over and pecked my unshaven cheek. "I'm Gloria, and you still haven't answered my question, Mr. Poet. Are going to take me home or not?"

I ordered us a couple of tequila shots and hunched over, trying to conceal my erection. "Assuming this isn't bullshit," I said.

"It's not bullshit," said Gloria, touching my knee. "You read this poem at The Poor Man's Cup one night, and I've wanted to meet you since. It was a poem about a flagpole.

I thought it was sexy, in a Freudian way. I'm a psych major."

"I know the poem you're talking about," I said. At the time, I had written what I considered to be two major poems that I read every time there was an open mic reading at The Poor Man's Cup. The first poem was a six-page scathing indictment of campus cliques—excluding, of course, my own clique of *artistes* and pseudo-intellectuals, who where beyond my reproach. The poem was titled "Bring in the Clowns," and I added a new verse, a new indictment of a different campus group each time I read it, to keep it fresh. I even wrote disparaging verse about frat guys, conveniently overlooking the fact that I was one. I envisioned "Bring in the Clowns" becoming the next "Howl," being read aloud by budding poets and heady lit majors on late nights in smoky dorm rooms.

The second poem in my oeuvre, the one Gloria was referring to, was about my first kiss in the sixth grade called "A Kiss at a Cold Flagpole." The poem boiled over with clichéd Freudian symbols, as Gloria pointed out, and ended with the speaker kissing a girl with "rosebuds for breasts." With a raging erection—similar to the one I had at that moment—the speaker looks up in the winter sky and "spots splashes of seminal white light."

I took the tequila shot, then ran my hand over my hair again. "It is *one* of my better poems," I told Gloria and offered her a cigarette.

"So what do you say, Mr. Poet? Are you taking me home?"

"I think an arrangement can be worked out."

I watched Gloria from behind when she got up to use the bathroom, her long legs strutting down a narrow hallway in a pair of tight-fitting blue jeans with rips in the thighs and knees. I had finally been dealt a good hand—at least a full house.

Or so I thought.

Paul—the middle-aged bartender with a thick black mustache—pointed to my empty glass. "You need another one, Ham?"

"I do."

"What about the lady?" he asked. He had a cool laid-back style where he could communicate solely by raising his bushy black eyebrows—a practical skill for a bartender.

"I know," I said. "I think this is the real deal."

"Then you better buy the lady a drink, buck," he said as cool as jazz. *Just to be sure*, his eyebrows added.

A full beer was waiting for Gloria when she got back from the bathroom. She had put on perfume and applied some stop-sign red lipstick. "You got me a beer," she said and kissed my cheek, leaving an oily red smear that she wiped with a cocktail napkin.

I lifted my drink—not a toast exactly, but one of those vague and impassive male gestures. I took a cigarette from my pack and handed it to Gloria. I was trying to make it seem like a strange girl hitting on me was as commonplace as laundry, to make it seem like it was just another day the life of a poet. I was trying to make it seem like I didn't have a hard-on.

Gloria lit the Winston. "After these drinks, let's leave."

I raised my beer glass again. "No bullshit?"

She leaned in close and gave my balls a gentle squeeze, and I saw splashes of seminal white light behind the bar.

"Paul, I'll take my tab."

Gloria's apartment was tiny—two rooms and a bathroom in a communal housing complex similar to my own only

more modern and maintained than mine. Despite being
small, the living room was decorated Gatsby-esque with
a lavish white sofa and a hand-knit white afghan thrown
over the back. A large coffee table with a white marble surface stood in front of the sofa. On a bookshelf that nearly
touched the ceiling, there was a framed studio portrait of a
handsome, affluent-looking couple hugging, smiling while
staring deep into each other's eyes. Beside it was another photo of a long-haired Gloria and three girls—all in
graduation gowns—standing in front of a flagpole. But the
gaudiest artifact in the apartment hung on the wall above
the sofa. Someone had painted a horrible still life in oils of
a naked woman sprawled on a divan, coyly twirling a lock
of black hair around her index finger. The woman looked
vaguely like Gloria—if Gloria had suffered a stroke and
became paralyzed on the right side of her face. It was the
type of tacky art that made "A Kiss at a Cold Flagpole" look
probing and profound.

I sat down as Gloria walked into the bedroom where
she had cold beer in a small refrigerator. My hands were
sweating, and the beer and tequila churned in my stomach.
Gloria came back and handed me a can of Miller Light
then she turned on the radio with a remote control. She
played Hootie and the Blowfish and started singing along
in a croaky, off-key voice.

For the first time in almost two hours, I lost my erection.

Gloria began rubbing my thigh, and I froze. I couldn't
stop staring at the couple gazing longingly into each other's
eyes, who I assumed were her parents, nor could I forget
the fact that "Hold My Hand" was puking out the speakers.
While I hated the album, I knew "Hold My Hand" would
be followed "Let Her Cry," and I didn't know if I could
take it. A guy I lived with in the fraternity house listened

to Hootie and the Blowfish, literally, six to ten hours a day, and I had developed a physical aversion to it; the symptoms included muscle tenseness and headaches and infrequent dry heaves. Listening to Hootie and the Blowfish, to this very day—almost twenty years later—is a sadistic form of torture for me.

Of course, Gloria couldn't have known this as she grabbed the back of my head and drilled her tongue into my mouth. I pulled away and glanced over my shoulder. "That's an interesting painting," I said.

"My ex-boyfriend painted it. It's me."

"So he's a painter."

"Yes." Gloria had little use for the conversation, so she employed Plan B, which was to pull me on top of her and grab my crotch.

It worked.

My erection returned like a stampeding cavalry, and we began dry humping beneath the naked painting of the long-haired stroke victim.

I unbuttoned her jeans and plunged my hand inside her panties. She wasn't just wet, she was gushing. It then occurred to me that Gloria was quite possibly a nymphomaniac, like one of the college girls in the B-movies, and she couldn't care less about my poem, but at that moment, it didn't matter.

She was unzipping my fly when I was overwhelmed with the need to piss. Each time her hand inadvertently pressed against my groin, it felt as if she were poking my bladder with a safety pin. "I have to go to bathroom," I whispered into her ear.

"Quick, Ham," she gasped, a circle of our combined saliva glistened around her mouth like clown make-up. "I need you inside me."

I sprinted through the dark bedroom and into the bathroom, running my hand across the wall, searching for the
light switch. I found it and glanced in the mirror, giving
myself the thumbs up as I tried to pee. However, I couldn't.
My erection wouldn't waver, and I wasn't about to stand in
the shower. I was stricken, again, by my inability to urinate
in a strange place, a life-long problem. So I waited, and
waited, and tried to think about other things.

And I waited.

And while I waited for my boner to go down and the
urine to flow, Gloria waited for me, pulsating on the sofa.
Finally, I gave up and went back into the living room.

When I returned, Gloria was as naked as the stroke victim on the divan. She had one leg propped up on the coffee
table, and her head was tossed back as her fingers jitterbug-
ged in a patch of black pubic hair. I stood dumbly in the
doorway.

"Don't you want to fuck me?" she asked, trying to make
her voice throaty.

I nodded like an idiot. "Yes, please."

"Then come on, Mr. Poet. Fuck me."

I started by kissing her breasts and worked my mouth
down to her navel. The discomfort of having to urinate disappeared as I went down on her. She grabbed the back of
my hair and ground her pelvis into my nose. I licked like
a dog lapping up a spill, hoping that I'd eventually hit the
sensitive spot. Then I did, and she started moaning loud-
er, moaning and grinding her hips. Her thighs started to
spasm.

Then the sound of a rusty zipper ripped opening was followed by a warm blast of air. My head snapped back, and
I knocked my skull against the white marble top on the
coffee table. *Bam!* And down went Ham the Man. Curled

into a fetal position on the floor, I clutched my head and again spotted splashes of seminal white light.

I didn't know what to say. I closed my eyes as a lump that would grow to the size of a golf ball by the morning started to form on the back of my head. I was embarrassed—for me, for Gloria, for the entire evening, for the stupid poem that got us here and my entire stupid life of posturing as a poet. It was all bullshit.

Finally, I glanced up at Gloria. She was covering her face with her hands, a naked tableau of shame below the naked painting above her.

"I guess I should be going," I said, standing up without an erection. "Running from an Angel" was on, and had things been any different—any less tragic—I might've laughed at the irony. Instead, I grabbed my jacket and let the words that I wanted to say to Gloria roll around like pills in my mouth. I wanted to rub her back and tell her it was all right. I wanted to tell her what I couldn't tell myself, but I didn't.

"I'm sorry," I said, my hair falling in pieces on my face.

"Just leave," she said. So I did.

Outside her apartment, the air was humid as the morning and the soggy notions of summer approached. I stuffed my hands in my pockets, surprised at how sober I had become following what I would one day describe to my grad school friends as "The Blast."

The walk back to my apartment led me through a residential neighborhood, and I stopped to piss behind some bushes in the front yard of a large white colonial. All the lights were off, its occupants soundly asleep. A steady stream of pent-up urine beat against the dirt.

I finished, zipped up, and noticed a dark puddle of urine running from my thigh to the hem of my jeans. Piss-soaked, I thought about writing a poem about the night then decided to write a story instead. It was then that I realized I was a better fit for fiction.

1996
THE TAO OF DOLTON

BIG RAY AND WIGGY were spitting tobacco juice at each other so Doug and I hit the deck, taking cover behind the couch as the globs of brown gunk lobbed overhead.

"Cut the shit, you hicks!" Doug grabbed a cushion and held it like a shield in front of him as Big Ray and Wiggy kept spitting, missing each other and splattering the walls and the dumpy brown carpet.

It was Thursday night, two months before graduation, and we were drinking beer and watching some 70s porn-flick where a coked-up and rail-thin blonde was masturbating with a giant black dildo. The spitting started when Wiggy, unprovoked, told Big Ray that his Ford truck would bitch slap Big Ray's Chevy—I had learned from living with them for almost two semesters that any comments about the other's truck were fighting words. Big Ray, his bottom lip bulging with Skoal, hocked a mouthful of brown juice at Wiggy. Wiggy retaliated, and the war was on.

"Cut the shit," Doug yelled again, pulling himself up from the floor as Big Ray and Wiggy reloaded their bottom lips. "Maybe you animals from Bum-fuck, Maine, sit around and spit at each other, but civilized human beings do not! This is unnatural, *inhuman*! Have you forgotten that Ham and I also pay rent here?"

Doug's face was puffy and red. A ringer for a young Paul Simon, pale and elfish, Doug's daintiness made it near-impossible for a couple of boys the size of Big Ray and Wiggy to see his anger as anything but comedic.

Big Ray stared at Doug, long and steady, like a baseball closer glaring at his catcher for a sign. He then tugged on the brim of his baseball cap and drove his index finger up his left nostril. Then, in one fluid motion, he withdrew the finger and flicked a snot the size of his thumbnail at Doug. It blasted Doug square in the chest, a bull's eye, lodging to his polo shirt.

Doug sprung from the couch and screamed, performing an apoplectic jig on the dip-stained carpet as he swatted at the snot. "Oh my God, oh my God!" Doug bolted into his bedroom, which was off the living room, and slammed the door behind him.

"What crawled up the hermaphrodite's ass?" Big Ray shrugged.

Wiggy shook his head. Wiggy's real name was Eric, but according to the story related to me by Big Ray, when Wiggy was in junior high, he was slow to hit puberty. Being a tall kid, he was teased relentlessly by a group of guys in his gym class for not having sprouted pubic hair yet. Tired of the taunting, Wiggy cut a patch of brown hair from a wig he found in the attic of his parents' farmhouse and super-glued it on his pubic area, fooling no one. Naturally reticent, he was tagged with the nickname Wiggy, which followed him, along with Big Ray, to college in New Hampshire where we all—including Doug—had joined

Alpha Delta Delta in the same pledge class. After living in the same communal housing complex as juniors, we decided to room together for our senior year and rented a place in a large dilapidated Victorian that a slumlord had converted into three separate student apartments that he barely maintained. As far as personalities were concerned, however, Big Ray and Wiggy couldn't have been more different than Doug and me.

Big Ray and Wiggy grew up in a small town in upstate Maine called Dolton. Bordering Canada, Dolton was one of those xenophobic towns of 400 residents, plucked straight from a Stephen King novel. The town was named after its founder, Herb Dolton. In 1802, the town was chartered on a strict, oppressive Christian doctrine, and Herb, a minister, was named the town's first mayor. Shortly afterward, in 1805, Herb fell from grace when he was tried, convicted, and eventually exiled for having sex with a pig. The damning evidence: one of Herb's sows gave birth to a piglet that townsfolk claimed looked like the mayor. If you look it up, you'll find it in the town's records. To this day, the Doltons' lineage lingers in the town, although the "pig-fuckers" are rarely seen in public, living in trailers on the outskirts. Big Ray and Wiggy said they went to elementary school with Chuck Dolton, who never made it past the fifth grade. However, both Big Ray and Wiggy concurred that Chuck looked like someone whose family might've "humped a few hogs along the way."

In many ways, Big Ray and Wiggy became Dolton's Lewis and Clark. Few Doltonians ever leave the town for any reason, other than to fight in foreign wars, and the family trees had an unfortunate tendency to not branch off. When Big Ray and Wiggy were recruited from their regional high school to play on the offensive line for our small Division III college, they were sent off as heroes, complete with a going away party at the V.F.W.

But they brought with them their Doltonian way of life—marked by bombproof calmness and simple, minimalist pleasures—which was as foreign to someone like Doug, who grew up in Glenn Falls, New York, as listening to contemporary jazz was to Big Ray and Wiggy.

At that time, I was still carving out an identity for myself, trying to figure out what Ham the Man wanted to do with the rest of his life. In a few short months, I would have a bachelor's degree in English writing, and other than having a vague notion that I might someday want to write books, I had no clue what I wanted to do otherwise. My immediate plans were to move home with my parents after graduation, where my father had been slightly pacified by the fact that I finally cut my **GIRL HAIR**. Nonetheless, due in large part to my lack of vision and direction, coupled with the uncertainty of the future, my anxiety was amplified, and I had started having panic attacks that winter. I became paralyzed by my fears of the future and some days struggled to get out of bed by noon.

Doug came back into the living room wearing a different pressed polo shirt with his hair freshly gelled and his composure regained. He sat next to me on the couch, pretending to not to notice Big Ray and Wiggy, who were grinning at him.

"Hey, Dougie, have you ever spooned with another dude?" Big Ray asked.

Doug flinched but didn't take the bait. "So, Ham," he said, turning to me, "who was the girl that called earlier?"

"She's someone from my Women's Lit class," I said. "We're going out tomorrow night."

"Is she good-looking?" Big Ray asked.

I nodded solemnly, for it was a solemn issue. The girl, Allison, was by far the most sensible and intelligent woman who had ever agreed to go on a date with me. After three and a half years of mistakes, misfires and misadventures with women, I had finally landed a date with a smart and beautiful girl—**A KEEPER**, as my father would say—who literally made me tingle when I was around her.

"Better be careful, Ham," Big Ray said to me.

"Why?"

"Pa always told me to watch out for the pretty ones. He said if a woman looks that good, she probably stinks like hornpout. He always tells me nothing is ever as good as it looks and be wary of things that look too good." Big Ray spit in the beer bottle he was holding.

Wiggy nodded.

"That is retarded logic," Doug said. "I've been with plenty of good-looking girls, and they've smelled fine. In fact, more than fine. Don't listen to this idiot, Ham."

"What about you, Dougie?" asked Big Ray. "Being a hermaphrodite and all, I figured you'd know it from both sides?"

Doug huffed then sighed. For the entire time we lived together, Doug had absorbed hermaphrodite jokes like a tank takes bullets. And though Doug bragged of an impressive sexual resume, we had never actually seen him bring home a woman, or a man, for that matter. In that sense, he reminded me of my old manager at the pizza place, although Doug didn't share the same affinity for Michael Bolton.

"Remember, Ham," Doug said, "these comments are coming from the same animal who changes his underwear once a week."

"I once went twenty-seven days without changing my shorts." Big Ray folded his large arms across his chest and leaned back in his chair. "I won a contest."

"You didn't win," Wiggy said. "Billy Fenton won, and I came in second."

"You're a goddamn liar," Big Ray said and spit at Wiggy, missing and hitting the wall behind him. "I won that contest."

Wiggy shook his head. "Nope."

Big Ray stood up from his chair and pointed at Wiggy. "All right, you Ford-driving motherfucker, let's go put on a clean pair of shorts and settle this once and for all. The loser has to wear the other's dirty shorts for a week."

"You're on," Wiggy said and stood up. The two men, chest-to-chest, stared at each other like boxers receiving their instructions.

Not able to suppress his grin, Big Ray gave Wiggy a small, but forceful shove. "I'm going to destroy you," he said.

Doug ran his hands through his hair. "You're both inhuman. Animals. Seriously. Animals."

I sold weed to make ends meet my senior year. Part of the reason I cut my hair was to look inconspicuous, but I'm sure dealing drugs did little to assuage my panic attacks. I was moving a couple of ounces a week that I got from Pete, who was supplying weed for a good portion of the campus by that point. While I was still small enough to keep me off the police's radars, it was enough cash to pay a good chunk of my rent, keep a head bag and take Allison to a four-star French restaurant in the White Mountains.

When I picked up Allison at her apartment that night, she was wearing a slinky black dinner dress and toeless black heels. Her straight blond hair was clipped back, exposing a long stretch of smooth white neck. Rarely had I seen her outside of our Women's Lit course, where she wore sensible sweaters and long flowing paisley skirts. The transformation was startling, and I tingled all over.

"You look ravishing," I said as we walked to my car. "Seriously, you look great."

"Aren't you the perfect gentleman caller," Allison said with a feigned Southern drawl.

"I have reservations at a French restaurant but we can bag it for KFC if you'd like to connect to your Southern roots," I said.

"I'd hate for you to break the reservations."

"Do you know what types of food French restaurants serve?" I asked. It was an honest question. With the exception of chicken cordon bleu and French onion soup, I couldn't think of a single French dish.

Allison shrugged as I opened the passenger door. "I'm not sure," she said, "but I know they have good wine."

We arrived at the restaurant and were seated in the back at a small candle-lit table for two covered with white linen and crystal water glasses. The lightning was dim and in the corner, an arm's length from our table, two mustached men in tuxedos played soft violins.

Our waiter approached the table, and as soon as I recognized him, I groaned and turned my head in the other direction. It was Michael Ladd, a handsome son of a bitch who had been in my fiction writing class the previous semester. After I abandoned my poetic persona the previous year, I went back to being boring. But a genuine interest in learning to write had been sparked, and in the fall, I enrolled in a fiction writing class, thinking the fiction writers would be less pretentious and dramatic than poets. While this—in my life anyway—has proved generally true, Michael Ladd was the exception.

If you put a pen in Michael Ladd's hand and his cock on a chopping block and told the guy to string together a decent sentence, he'd be doomed to a dick-less life. Yet this didn't stop him from adopting a finely-honed professorial literary persona. To begin with, he wrote his stories using the byline M.S. Ladd, thinking it sounded more literary. Again, in my experiences, writers who use their initials without a good reason are generally dick-holes.

On top of this, M.S. Ladd would wear a blazer and blue jeans to every class and sit in the corner of the room with his wire-rimmed reading glasses pushed up on his forehead, scratching his face and offering canned criticism: "These characters need to breath" or "The story lacks confluence." In short, M.S. Ladd represented everything that still makes me sick about the literary community.

At the restaurant, however, instead of the literary blazer, he stood at our table in a dress shirt and a black bowtie with his hands folded behind his back. "I never expected to ever see *you* here," he said to me with disgust and disdain. M.S. Ladd thought as highly of me as did of him.

"If it isn't M.S. Ladd, the literary tour de force," I said. "I guess you're waiting tables until the check for your Guggenheim fellowship comes in."

"I make great money here," he said with a smug smile.

I was tempted to tell him that I made decent money—without the monkey suit—dealing bud and never leaving my apartment, but he had already turned his attention to Allison, flashing her one of his soap-opera smiles. "Good evening, Allison."

"Hello, Michael," she said and waved with her fingers. "I didn't know you worked here."

"Indeed," he said and bent at the waist—the motherfucker

actually used the word *indeed*. "Can I get you something to drink, *mademoiselle*?"

"I'll have the Barolo," she said. I glanced at the wine-list and gulped. I was going to have to sell a lot of green for that glass of wine.

"Exquisite choice," he said, keeping his back to me. "How about you?"

"Coors Light," I said. "By the way, do you work on tips?"

He shot me a dirty look and left the table. I was pretty sure he wouldn't spit in my drink; he didn't have the balls.

"I see you know the great M.S. Ladd," I said "That pompous asshole was in my fiction writing class last semester."

"He is a little full of himself. We went out once," Allison said.

I tried to look interested, or at least polite, as a fist-sized ball of bile bounced around my gut. "You went out with M.S. Ladd? What in the world would make you go out with M.S. Ladd?"

"I heard he had a big penis."

It was as if I had been snap-punched in the windpipe. Bug-eyed, I waited for the corners of her lips to crack or her nose to involuntarily twitch, some small tell, anything to indicate that she was bluffing. But she remained stone-faced, sipping from her water glass. I bowed my head.

"Ham, are you all right?" Allison placed her hand on my wrist. "You look pale."

Before I could reply, M.S. Ladd and his monster cock came back with our drinks. With my head hung and my eyes averted, I hoisted my beer to my lips and drained half.

M.S. Ladd asked, "Can I get you an appetizer?"

"Tequila," I said without looking up. "Please."

The next night, I walked into the kitchen as Big Ray, Wiggy and Doug were eating hot dogs at the card table. When we moved into the apartment that September, we didn't have a kitchen table so Wiggy and Big Ray stole a card table and four folding chairs from a church rectory after being court-ordered to perform community service for open container violations. They justified the theft by saying that Jesus didn't approve of gambling, claiming that the table and chairs where used largely for bingo nights.

Wiggy offered me a hot dog, and I waved my hands and shook my head. After a morning and afternoon of intermittent vomiting, my appetite hadn't returned. The date was a disaster. I got so hammered that M.S. Ladd had the pleasure of shutting me off and the maitre d' had to escort me to the parking lot. Allison then drove my car to my apartment and had her roommate pick her up. I hadn't expected a call from her, and I didn't get one. In fact, I doubted she would ever talk to me again. I finally found a girl I liked, and I blew it with an irrational reaction to the news about M.S. Ladd's gargantuan appendage—another low for Ham the Man.

"You should see my shorts, Dougie," Big Ray said, his mouth stuffed with a half-masticated hot dog. "They've turned tan."

Doug said, "I'm eating."

Big Ray smirked. "Why are you getting worked up about my shorts, Dougie?"

Doug tried to change the subject. "You're quiet, Ham. How was your big date?"

"Terrible," I said, shaking another wave of nausea. "She had dated our waiter and started talking about his big cock.

I ended up getting really drunk."

"You shouldn't worry about those things," said Big Ray, wolfing down a fourth hot dog from the package of ten he split with Wiggy. "Imagine if you were Dougie. Not only is he a needle-dick, but he's got a cooze, too. Now those are some real problems."

"Fuck off," said Doug.

"And besides," Big Ray continued, "Pa says a big bunker-buster doesn't guarantee good results. He says it's the motion in the ocean that makes it."

"Maybe he's right," I said miserably.

"Damn straight." Big Ray nodded. "Or maybe Ma said that." He looked across the table at Wiggy. "What color are your shorts, Wig?"

Doug said, "I'm eating."

"Have they turned tan yet?"

"Not yet. Off-white, hinting at yellow."

Doug said, "I'm eating."

"Why are you always so uptight, Dougie?"

"Doesn't being filthy bother you? You're like …" Doug paused and squinted at his hands, as if the words he was searching for were printed on his palms. "You're, like, some kind of barn animal with no idea how to conduct yourself in a civilized society."

Big Ray stood up, unbuckled his belt then turned his back to Doug. With a swift, forceful tug, his jeans fell to his feet. If confirmation had been necessary, his briefs put an end to the discussion. His boxer shorts had, *indeed*, turned brownish, and I could smell them from across the kitchen. "Would you call these are tan or brown, Dougie," Big Ray asked with his head between his legs, staring at Doug.

Doug reached for the garbage can and started to heave up a hot dog as Big Ray and Wiggy exchanged a high-five.

Strangely, I started feeling a little better and reached for a beer in the fridge.

"That's a boy, Ham," Big Ray said, buckling his jeans. "Get back on that horse, kid."

⊕

After a week of standoffish behavior in class, out of no-where, Allison called me the next Friday afternoon—Day 10 of the underwear contest—and asked if I wanted to see a student production of Eugene O'Neill's *A Long Day's Journey into Night* with her. After the humiliation I endured after she spoke so frankly about M.S. Ladd's large quill, I told her I'd pick her up at six p.m.

As if the play wasn't depressing enough, on the ride home we listened to Jeff Buckley's *Grace*, a beautiful album that could turn a Christmas pageant into a suicide pact. Still, we were holding hands and flirting during the show—entirely inappropriate given the play's content—and we talked easily to one another on the car ride home. For the first time, I was genuinely enjoying the company of a female without scheming to get her in bed. Don't get me wrong, I was dying to get Allison in bed, but I was also happy to stick around and wait.

While parked in front her apartment, smoking a joint, we found ourselves snagged in an awkward silence, staring at one another and waiting for the other person to make a move, to tilt their head a smidgeon to one side and give the green light.

Then Allison spoke. "I need to ask you something, Ham," she said. While I thought she was going to ask me for a shot of wiper fluid to wash down with "My Last Goodbye," instead, she asked: "What happened the last time we went out? Why did you get so drunk?"

I shrugged and hung my head. "I couldn't handle the knowledge that M.S. Ladd, the worst person in the world, has a big penis," I said honestly. "But what was even worse was the thought of you and him…together. I mean, you're so fucking beautiful, and he's such a pretentious dick-hole."

"Is that what was bothering you?" She laughed. "If it makes you feel any better, I never slept with him. Not that it's any of your business, but I never, you know, saw *it*. My roommate Stephanie slept with him. She's the one who told me. I was only joking with you. I thought you knew."

"I'm an idiot," I said, slapping my forehead. "But that makes me feel better."

"Why are guys so hung up on penis size?"

"We grow up watching porn, and our egos are fragile. We assume bigger always means better."

"Men are idiots," Allison said, passing me the joint. "This is great pot, by the way. Do you know where I can get some?"

"It can probably be arranged."

While I was tapping out the roach in the car ashtray, Allison placed her hand on the back of my head and kissed me—a sneak attack—a soft kiss with lips pressed like pillows against mine. Then she pulled away and looked me in the eyes, her skin glowing in the green light of the radio's dial.

"Do you want to come inside?" she asked.

"Yes, please."

Allison lived with two other girls in a student-housing complex, a condominium with two floors and three modest-sized bedrooms—two upstairs and a smaller room off the kitchen. The place was clean and smelled of strawberries and lilacs and the faint scent of cigarettes. The furniture in

the living room was new, the floors vacuumed. The condominium stood in a stark contrast with my own apartment:
filthy and rundown and smelling of stale beer and sweaty
asses, not to mention the card table and the fold-up chairs
pilfered from a church; the cracked ceilings and the tobacco
juice stains on the walls, couches and carpets.

With her roommates out for the night, Allison and I
had the place to ourselves. She grabbed us a couple of Mi-
chelob bottles from the fridge, and we sat on the couch,
watching a *Discovery Channel* documentary on the two-
toed sloth—another aphrodisiac. While the two-toed sloth
snacked on tree bark and berries, we started making out.
The next thing I knew, I was on top of her, kissing her neck
and ear—pulling out all of the stops in my pathetic sexual
repertoire while trying not to seen overzealous.

"Do you want to go to my room?"

"Yes, please."

She took my hand and led me up the stairs to her bedroom. With the exception of a small pile of laundry beside
the bed, the room was spotless and meticulously organized.
While Allison used the bathroom, I scanned the pile of
laundry for her panties. I wanted to see them, the colors
and the cut. Briefly, under the spell of some self-destruc-
tive urge to mortify a woman whose company I was really
enjoying, I contemplated stealing a pair—a thought that
sadly thrilled me. Underwear, I realized, had become ubiq-
uitous in my life, establishing residency in all my thoughts,
which admittedly was stupid and perverse. But I couldn't
find a pair in the pile. If her panties were there, they were
at the bottom, hiding from me and my deviance.

Allison came back in the room, oblivious to my perver-
sion, and walked over to a portable stereo on her desk and
put on music. Hootie and the Blowfish.

Oh no.

Recalling the night with Gloria and The Blast, I began to get short of breath, my hands clamming up and limbs numbing—the first terrifying signs of an oncoming panic attack. The fact that I was extremely stoned wasn't helping matters.

"Ham, are you all right?" Allison asked, sitting beside me on the bed and placing her hand on my cheek. "What's wrong?"

"Could you turn off the music?" I started breathing heavily into my hands.

"Do you not like Hootie and the Blowfish?"

"It's a long story," I said between deep breaths.

"I didn't know." Allison got up and turned off the radio then came back to the bed and again sat beside me. "Better?"

"I'm having a panic attack," I said then lay back on her bed and rolled into a fetal position. I couldn't get my mind off the panic and dread and the physical symptoms it produced: heart palpitations, shortness of breath, dizziness and a dry mouth. I thought I was going to die of a heart attack, there on the bed, beside the coolest girl I'd ever met.

Allison, however, was familiar with panic attacks and handled it calmly. She told me that her mother suffered from them, and she got me a glass of water and a wet cloth for my forehead, talking me down in a soft soothing voice.

A half an hour later, humiliated, I was able to control breathing and sit up. Allison was watching the television in her room. She smiled at me. "Feeling better?"

"How are you able to do it, Allison?" I asked her.

"Do what? Watch television?"

For some reason, perhaps my perceived proximity to death, I was feeling whimsical and philosophical. "How can you be so calm with graduation coming and everything in the future so unsettled, so uncertain? How can you *not* be freaking out all of the time? I don't have a job lined up, do you?"

"I'm going to waitress this summer, but no, I don't have anything permanent lined up."

"Then why aren't you freaking out?"

"I am nervous," she said and clicked off the television. "And I'm scared and anxious and feeling vulnerable, but there's no point in freaking out. Life will go on, and I'll keep on living the best I can. I mean, what is the alternative? I suppose you can stick your head in an oven, or jump off a bridge, but I'd prefer to live. As shitty as life sometimes is, it beats being dead. But you're a writer, so it's normal for you to freak out. Writers freak out about everything."

"I haven't published anything."

"You're still a writer."

Allison and I lay on her bed that night, watching television, shooting the shit, and holding each other. I didn't try anything else and felt a steel plate of guilt weighing down my chest for ever wanting to steal her panties. As I was driving across campus that night, I admitted to myself that I could easily fall in love with Allison. That also scared the shit out of me.

When I walked into the kitchen the next morning, Big Ray and Wiggy were sitting in the fold-up chairs, shoulder to shoulder, an old newspaper splayed over the surface of the card table. On a wooden cutting board in front of Big Ray, there was a dead squirrel, its mouth open and its lifeless eyes, like scratched marbles, gazing at the ceiling. Big Ray's pocketknife glistened in his hand.

"What are you doing?" I asked.

"We're going to skin this squirrel that Wiggy shot and cook it in a stew," Big Ray said as he ran the blade of the knife lightly across his thumbprint. "Do you want some?"

Dried blood streamed from the hole in the squirrel's neck where the pellet had penetrated. "I think I'll pass."

"It tastes like chicken," Big Ray said. "Ain't that right, Wig?"

Wiggy turned to me. "Tastes like chicken."

"Then why not eat chicken?"

Big Ray shook his head like I'd asked him if he owned a gun, or why he refused to drink light beer. "When you shoot a critter, you use the meat, Ham. If you don't," he paused. "Well, that shit ain't right."

Wiggy nodded.

While I was consumed by fears of the unknown and anticipations of future torment, it also seemed that Allison was right: freaking out was preventing me from living. The Doltonians didn't struggle with anxieties or freak out about the future; they lived hand-to-mouth, in the moment. "Maybe I will try a bite," I said.

"That's a boy." Big Ray slapped me on the back as he turned the dead squirrel on its stomach with his other hand. Wiggy pressed down on its hind legs with both hands as Big Ray lifted the squirrel's tail then, with a deft horizontal stroke, slid the blade across its underside. "You got to skin her first," Big Ray said to me.

As the blade sliced through the muscle tissue, Doug walked into the kitchen, rubbing his eyes. "What is going on here?"

"We're skinning a squirrel, Dougie. Then we're going to fry up the meat and put it in a stew. You want some?" Big

Ray winked at Doug.

Doug looked at me. "Ham, tell me you're not eating this."

"I'm going to try it."

Doug's jaw hung open as he looked at me with shock and betrayal. "This is fucking *inhuman*! Squirrels are filthy animals. I can't believe what I'm seeing, Ham!"

Big Ray cleared his throat, now holding the squirrel by its hind legs. "It all goes in and comes out the same holes, Dougie."

And Wiggy said, "Damn straight."

In a last, desperate effort to hold onto the fragile balance of power in the apartment, Doug turned to me and shrugged.

"Damn straight," I said.

⊕

Squirrel tastes like chicken.

⊕

The stew set off an epiphany, a type of spiritual awakening that would make a snake handler jealous. After eating the squirrel, I began to live like the squirrel, fearing no missteps between branches or pellets in my path. I resigned myself to the simple stack of tasks that my days presented—nothing was too big or too small. They just were. I began to live like a Doltonian, and my panic attacks and my unfounded fears about the future vanished. My past mistakes and humiliations—"The Monkey Ring Rod," the STD's, "The Blast"—they were filed and forgotten for the moment. I began to take everything at face value and live in the present, eschewing metaphors, shunning labels. If something started to veer in the direction of strangeness, I accepted this for what it was. In this sense, through the boys from Dolton, I started to become an observer of the simple trials and terrors and joys of my fellow human beings, a skill that would serve me well when years later, I sat down and tried to write my first novel. And in my quiet moments, to this day, I'll sit still and repeat my mantra: *Damn straight, damn straight, damn straight.*

One Monday morning, I stopped for coffee at a shop in the student union building, and in the corner sat M.S. Ladd in the posture of Rodin's *The Thinker*. He held a copy *Ulysses* in front of his face, pitched at an angle so everyone in the coffee shop could see the cover and would be aware that he was reading Joyce. Spring had fully arrived, yet M.S. Ladd still wore his heavy tweed blazer, his blue jeans and penny loafers. I sat down at the table next to him and drank my coffee, flipping through *The Boston Globe*. M.S. Ladd peered at me over his book.

"I didn't see *you* here," he said with his wire-rimmed glasses resting on the tip of his nose.

"I'm here, M.S. Ladd."

"Like I said, I didn't notice," he said in a nasally, disaffected tone. "I'm afraid I was enraptured by one of the greatest works in the English language."

"You're reading *Cujo*?"

"I take it you've never read *Ulysses*."

"Nope. But I looked at the first page once," I said. "Right now I'm reading about The Red Sox, so I'll let you get back to your heady stuff." I whacked him on the back, tucked the paper under my arm and walked out with my coffee, whistling.

I could hear M.S. Ladd snort with disdain as I sung, "Damn straight."

⊕

For reasons I still don't understand, things with Allison cooled after the night of my Hootie-induced panic attack. Before the squirrel stew, I was too stubborn to call her. And she never called me. It was one of those games couples play when you don't want the other person to know that you're interested and you're trying to gauge their interest in you, watching the phone and waiting for it to ring. In class we'd smile crookedly at each other and wave, but we didn't speak again until the last class before final exams. Allison approached me in front of the English building where I was smoking a cigarette and asked if I wanted to go out for a beer. She was wearing a denim miniskirt that revealed a dangerous amount of tanned thigh, and like a man who had stepped in quicksand, I felt myself being swallowed by my old anxieties, regressing into Ham the Man.

We went to The Rusty Hammer, ordered a couple of beers and grabbed a table beneath the dartboard. Aside from a couple of local barflies, the pub was empty mid-afternoon.

Allison reached across the table and grabbed my hand. "Ham, you've seemed so relaxed lately. It's like something has come over you."

"I ate a squirrel."

"You did what?"

I cleared my throat. "My roommates shot a squirrel then cooked it in a stew. I had some and realized it tastes like chicken. It changed me."

Allison crossed and uncrossed then crossed her legs again. While I tried not to look, she caught me staring and grinned. "That's intriguing," she said. "I'd like to meet these guys. Where are they right now?"

"They're spearing suckers."

"They're what?"

"They sharpen tree branches into spears with their pocket knives then wait on the edge of a stream for these fish, called suckers, to swim by. When they see a sucker, they try to impale with the stick. I went with them last week. I didn't catch anything."

"Why would they do that?"

"They just do."

She reached under the table and squeezed my knee. "Why don't we go back to your place and wait for them?"

"Damn straight."

When Allison and I arrived at my apartment, Big Ray and Wiggy were in the living room watching a hunting program and spitting into beer cans. On the television, a bearded man in a fluorescent orange hunting vest had a buck in the crosshairs of the scope on his 30.06. With such high-drama, Big Ray and Wiggy didn't notice us enter.

"You got her," said Wiggy.

"Take her down, you son of a bitch," Big Ray urged the hunter.

The rifle fired, and the deer fell like a sack of sand to the ground. Allison screamed. Big Ray and Wiggy spun around.

"We didn't hear you come in," Big Ray said. When they saw Allison, he and Wiggy both stood up from the couch and took off their baseball caps. "Ma'am," Big Ray said and nodded to her.

"Ma'am," said Wiggy.

Allison waved, fanning her fingers. "I'm Allison."

"Good to meet you, Allison. I'm Ray, and this here is Eric." I had never heard Big Ray call Wiggy by his given name. "We're watching this hunting show if you folks would like to join us," he said.

"Where's Dougie?" I asked.

"At class," Big Ray said and looked at Allison. "He's a hermaphrodite."

Allison turned to me. "Is that true?"

"Yes."

Allison, however, didn't seem enthused by the first felled deer, so I begged off to my room. The next critter would have to meet its maker without us.

Now Ham the Man would have worked himself into a panic attack about whether he had anything potentially embarrassing laying around his bedroom—a jizz rag, a streaked pair of boxers, one of the ridiculous poems I used to write. But when we sat on my bed, I stretched out easily and allowed Allison to peruse my room. Not that there was much to see, other than a bed, a bookcase—double-shelved—a desk and a word processor. There was a pile of dirty laundry in the closet beside an old hope chest where I locked up my weed.

Allison sat down beside me and folded her hands on her lap. "So, Ham, do you think you can get me some of that pot?"

Without making a move toward the hope chest, I said, "I think it can be arranged." Then I turned and kissed her. Our hands worked wildly, rubbing and caressing, pulling off each other's shirts. I rubbed her thigh then slid my hands up her skirt, rubbing the warmth between her legs and slipping a finger beneath the elastic band on her panties. Her breath was hot on my neck.

What happened next had the texture of a nightmare.

Everything moved in slow motion; my limbs seemed too heavy to mobilize, too slow to react.

I wanted to go down on Allison, to make her tingle like I tingled when she was around me. I ran my tongue in a straight line from her neck to her breasts to her belly button, gently sliding her panties down her legs. My face was hovering over her silky blonde pubic hair when the bedroom door flew open.

Doug stood in the doorway, holding a tree branch shaved into a spear. A brownish-yellow piece of cloth hung off the end of the stick. Allison screamed, pulling down her skirt and covering her chest with a pillow. I jumped up from the bed, my fists raised.

"Look!" Doug yelled, pointing at the cloth. Two sets of heavy footsteps came thumping up the stairs behind him. "Look at these animals!"

Then Big Ray burst into the room with a towel tied around his waist and tackled Doug to the ground. The cloth flew off the stick, lobbing through the air, and landing on Allison's lap. She glanced at the underwear, her face frozen like she'd being shot in the gut. When she figured out what it was touching her skin, she threw back her head and let loose a blood-curdling, high-pitched B-movie scream.

"I'm really sorry about this, ma'am. I'm sorry, Ham," Big Ray said, hurriedly snatching his stained briefs from the floor and pushing Doug and Wiggy out of my bedroom, slamming the door behind him.

Allison sat on the edge of my mattress, her face buried in her hands.

"I'm so sorry, Allison," I said, putting my arm around her shoulder.

She lifted her head, and I noticed she was laughing, not sobbing or hiding her face. "Was that the hermaphrodite?"

she asked.

"Yeah."

"That was pretty gross, Ham," she said, resting her head on my shoulder. "It was some sort of ugly."

"You might be the coolest person I've ever met."

And she was. And she is. After seventeen years of marriage and two children, we'll sometimes laugh remembering Big Ray's briefs, my conversion to a Doltonian, the ugliness that framed our courtship. "You should write about it, Ham," Allison will say to me.

"Who would want to read about that crap? It was college," I'll say.

"You'd be surprised. There's some beauty in all that ugliness. And it made you the writer you are today."

"I fucking love you, Allison."

⊕

The next morning, after Allison left, I emerged from my bedroom. Big Ray and Wiggy were sitting at the card table holding large plastic cereal bowls filled with Captain Crunch and whole milk. They each had a beer in front of them. Doug was sitting on the counter, also drinking a beer. We were graduating in a week after our final exams, and we had to be out of the apartment by the following Monday.

"Listen, Ham. I'm sorry," Big Ray said. "We didn't mean to barge in on you like that. But that son of a bitch stole my shorts." He pointed at Doug.

"Someone else had to see them," said Doug.

"No worries," I said, reaching into the fridge for a beer.

"Wiggy and I called the contest a draw," said Big Ray. "We're going to start another tomorrow at high noon."

"This is unbelievable," said Doug. "I'm leaving."

"Don't keep your boyfriend out too late," said Big Ray.

"Fuck off," Doug said brusquely as he walked out of the kitchen. Moments later, the front door slammed behind him.

Big Ray put his hand on my back and looked at me as solemn as a monk. "That girl sure is looker, Ham."

"Damn straight," I said.

"Listen, I got to know, Ham. What did it smell like down there?" He and Wiggy turned to me at the same time, waiting on my response.

I paused then said, smirking, "Like hornpout."

"Goddamn it, Pa was right," Big Ray said.

"Damn straight," I said.

"Damn straight, Ham. You're the man," Big Ray said as he raised his beer.

"No," I said, shaking my head and toasting. "I'm just Ham."

☯

ACKNOWLEDGMENTS

I would like to acknowledge the following places—some of which have long stopped publication—where these pieces were originally published, in vastly different forms, many moons ago: *Defenestration*, *The Dublin Quarterly*, *Front & Centre*, and *Air in the Paragraph Line*.

I'd also like to thank Matthew Guerruckey, who resurrected this manuscript, encouraged me to revise these pieces for his site *Drunk Monkeys* and continued to believe in this little book. Few people would put their faith in a story about a queef, but you wouldn't be reading this right now if it weren't for Matt and his new baby, Marginalia Publishing. I'd also like to thank Pamela Langley for her help editing and lending a female perspective to the manuscript.

Thanks to Paul and Kenny for allowing us to use the pic.

There are also a few old friends, in particular, worthy of a nod: Pete (you remember!), Todd (can I use your head as a high-hat?), Micah (you can't really grow a beard on your nose!), Phish (best morning cough I've ever heard), Rocco (my life is *your* fault!), Pee Wee (my Natty Light brother), Father Rob (you're *hahd*-core!), Big Jay (let's go to Canada) and my Sig-Ep brothers and friends from PSC—now PSU—in the 90s.

Of course, none of this gets done without the love and support of my wife Liz and my kids, Paige and Owen. I hope it is a very, very, *very* long time until my children read *Some Sort of Ugly*. I'm not ready to answer their questions yet and may never have an adequate explanation for some of these tales.

NATHAN GRAZIANO lives in Manchester, New Hampshire. He is the author of three collections of poetry—*Not So Profound* (Green Bean Press, 2003), *Teaching Metaphors* (sunnyoutside, 2007) and *After the Honeymoon* (sunnyoutside, 2009)—a collection of short stories, *Frostbite* (Green Bean Press, 2002), and several chapbooks of fiction and poetry. He also writes a Red Sox column for *Dirty Water News* in Boston. A chapbook of short prose pieces titled *Hangover Breakfasts* was published by Bottle of Smoke Press in 2012. For more information, visit his website at www.nathangraziano.com or his blog www.nathangraziano.blogspot.com.

www.ingramcontent.com/pod-product-compliance
Lightning Source LLC
Chambersburg PA
CBHW071344130626
46556CB00005B/2019